Circle Square

Greenwillow Books, *An Imprint of* HarperCollins*Publishers*

By Kelly Bingham

Pictures by Paul O. Zelinsky

For Marty, my ♡—K. B.

To my family of squares—P. O. Z.

Circle, Square, Moose

For information address HarperCollins Children's Books,
a division of HarperCollins Publishers,
195 Broadway, New York, NY 10007.
www.harpercollinschildrens.com

Mixed media were used to prepare the full-color art.
The text type is Geometric 212 Book.

Library of Congress Cataloging-in-Publication Data

Bingham, Kelly L., (date)
Circle, square, Moose / by Kelly Bingham ; pictures by Paul O. Zelinsky.
pages cm
"Greenwillow Books."
Summary: When Zebra and his enthusiastic friend Moose are asked
to exit a book about shapes, Moose has other plans.
ISBN 978-0-06-229003-8 (trade ed.)—ISBN 978-0-06-229004-5 (library bdg.)
[1. Shape—Fiction. 2. Moose—Fiction. 3. Zebras—Fiction.
4. Behavior—Fiction. 5. Friendship—Fiction.
6. Humorous stories.] I. Zelinsky, Paul O., illustrator II. Title.
PZ7.B51181685Ci 2014 [E]—dc23 2013019534

14 15 16 17 18 SCP 10 9 8 7 6 5 4 3 2 1
First Edition

Greenwillow Books

Shapes

are all around us. We see them every day. Have you ever looked at a button?

This one is a . . .

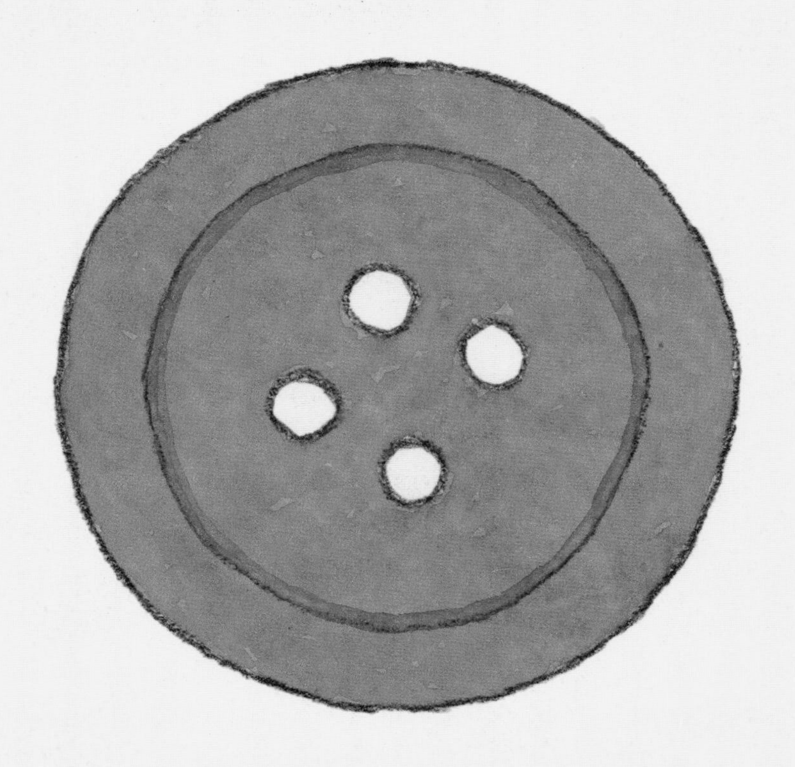

circle.

What about that sandwich you had for lunch?

That is a . . .

square.

And if you look closely at a square
will see that it is made of four equ

Look—this is a book about shapes. Not animals. You are in the wrong book.

And please put that sandwich back. It's our square.

Now, let's learn about

triangles.

Do you know what a triangle is?

A **TRIANGLE** is . . .

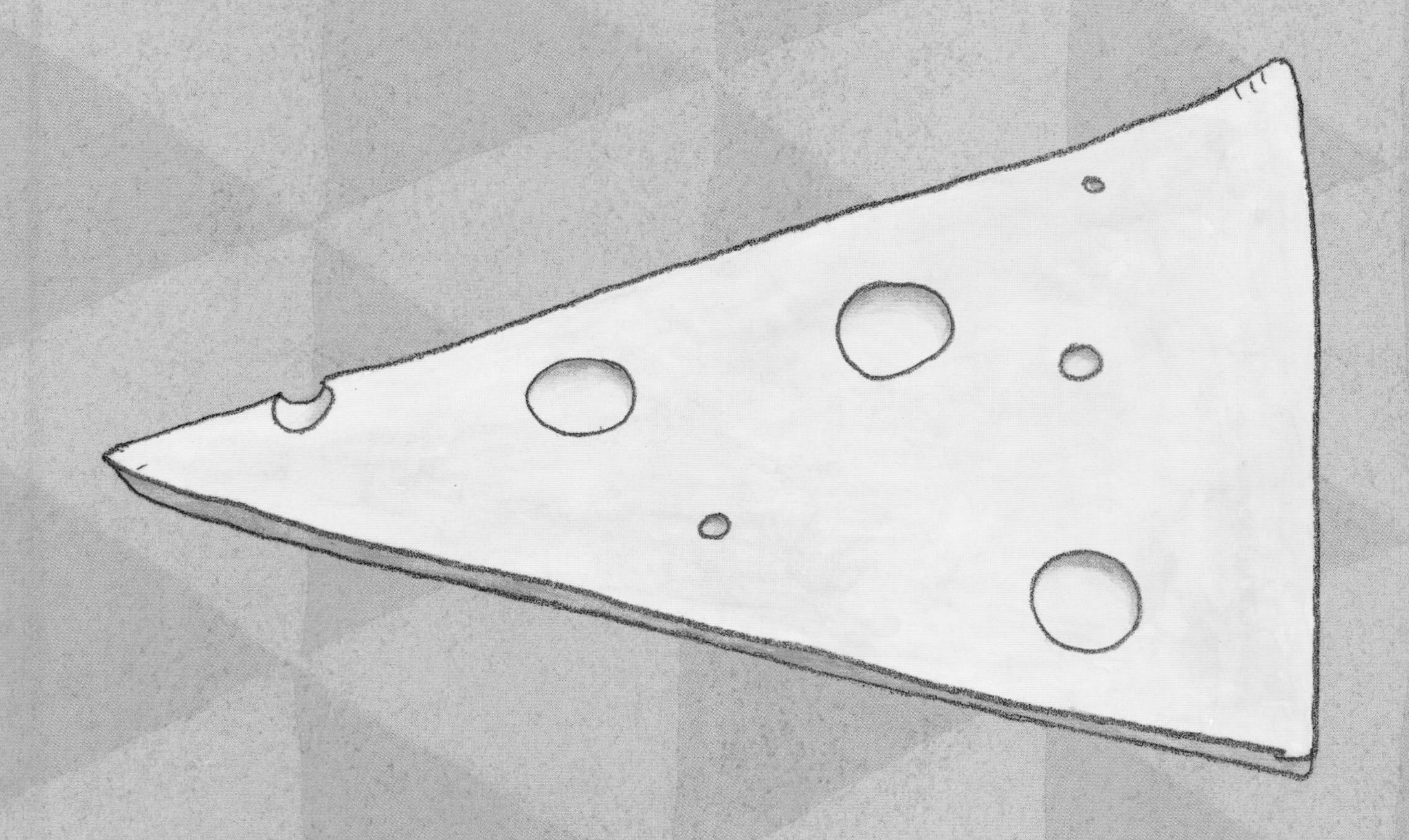

A wedge of cheese

A piece of pie

Or ears like these!

Cute, but this is not an animal book.
It is a shape book. You both need to leave.

Let's talk about rectangles!

A **RECTANGLE** is . . .

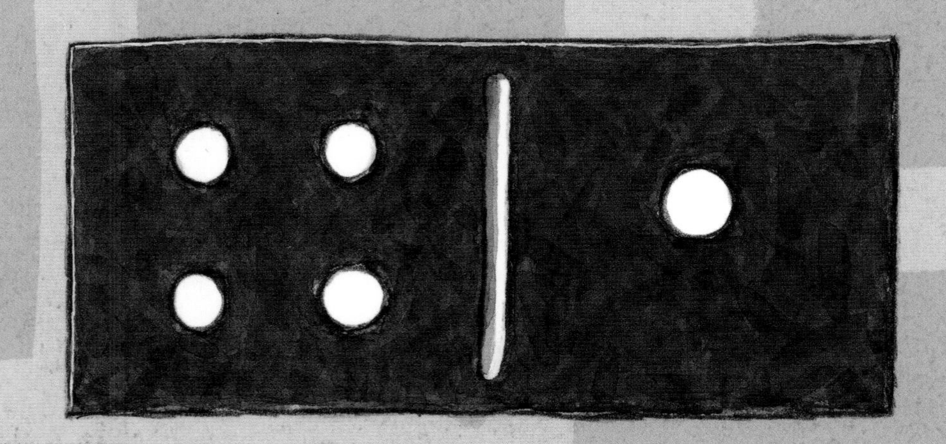

A domino

A book

to read

And a ~~tall window~~ Moose

A **DIAMOND** is . . .
The shape in a crown

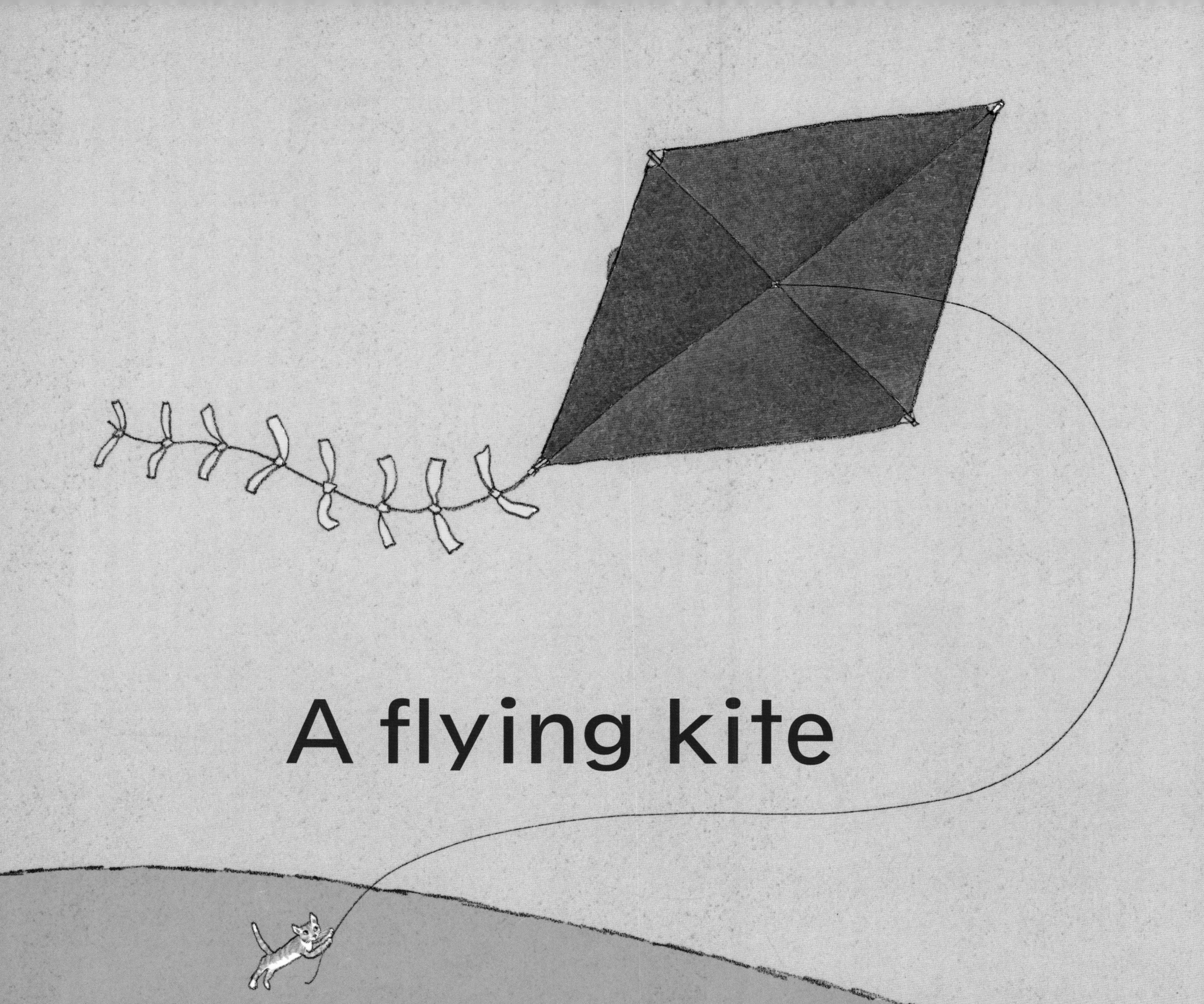

A flying kite

And
a
~~sign~~
~~to~~
~~slow~~
~~down~~
Moose
SLOW
Get down!

Okay. You have to leave. You are ruining the book

This is a bo

about shap

I'll handle this.

Psst! Moose! Come on!
NO!

Time to
leave now!

No!

A **SQUARE** is . . .

A pretty picture frame

A shiny tile

Or a fun board game

What is a curve?

A **CURVE** *might* be . . .

A snake-ity snake

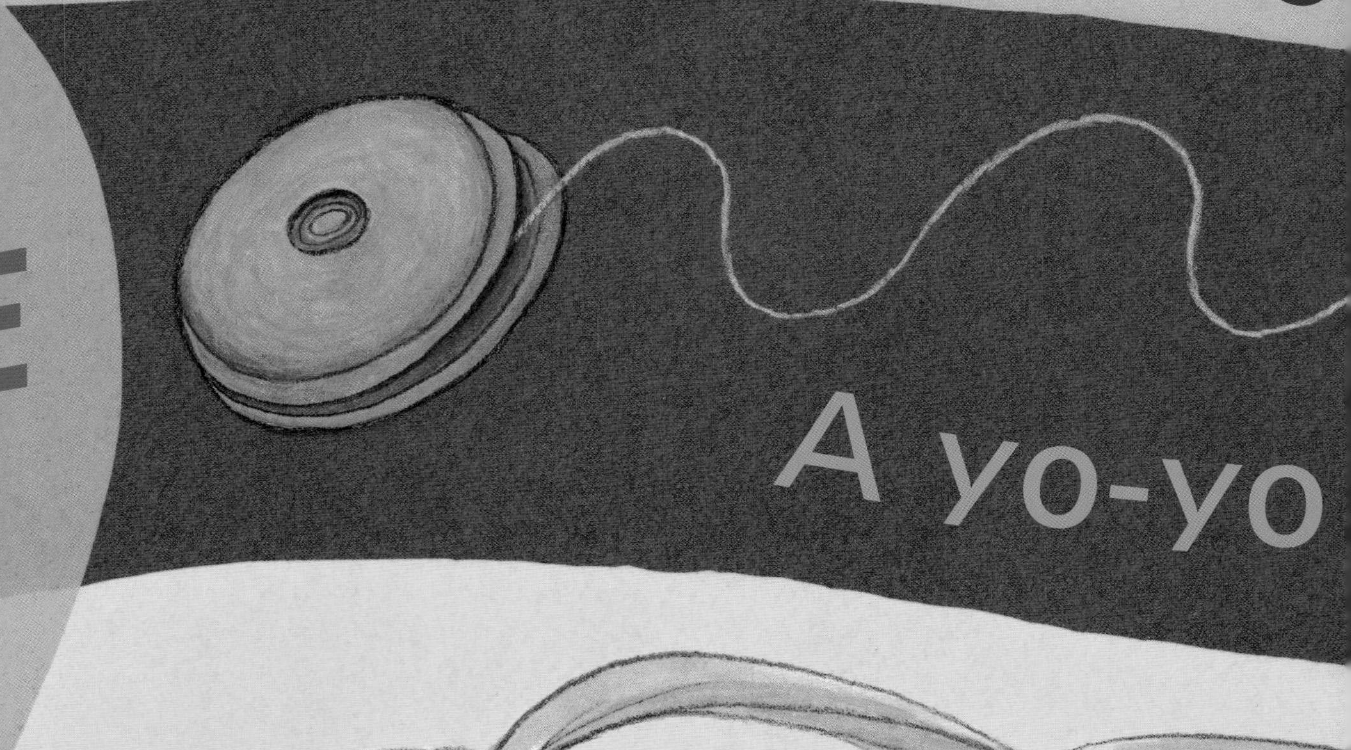

A yo-yo

trick
Or a ribbon’s wake

Uh-oh.

Enough.
Everyone out.
I can't! I think I'm stuck!
But I love shapes!

GO!
Uh...
a little help?
Moose?

A CIRCLE IS ROUND.

A **CIRCLE** is . . .

A polka dot

Help!

A lollipop
Hold on!
The sun
so hot
Hurry!

Don't worry, Zebra. I'll handle this.
The su
so hot

Circles also make HOLES.
The sun so hot
M-o-o-o...
...O-O-O-S-E!
Coming!

THAT'S IT. I'M DONE. GOOD-BYE. YOU CAN FINISH THIS BOOK YOURSELVES
Good.

Moose! We ruined the book.

We can finish this. There's only one shape left. The star.
That's my favorite shape!

But now we won't get to hear the rhyme.

Zebra. Trust me.

A STAR

is for Zebra,
my very good friend.

Zebra and Moose.
Friends
to the
end.

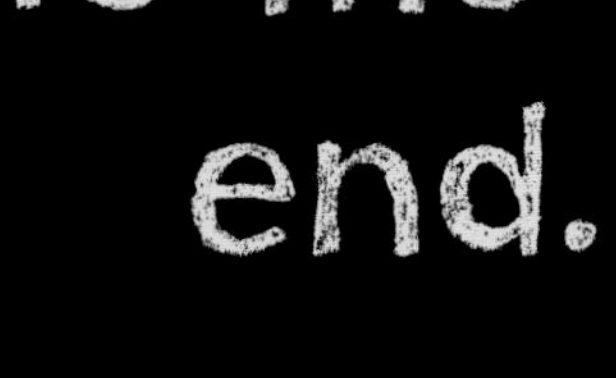

Thank you, Moose.

You're welcome.

The End

Can we do that again?

Yes, Zebra.
We can do that
again.